W9-BUI-759

Claus, S.
TOP SECRET
DO NOT OPEN TIL XMAS

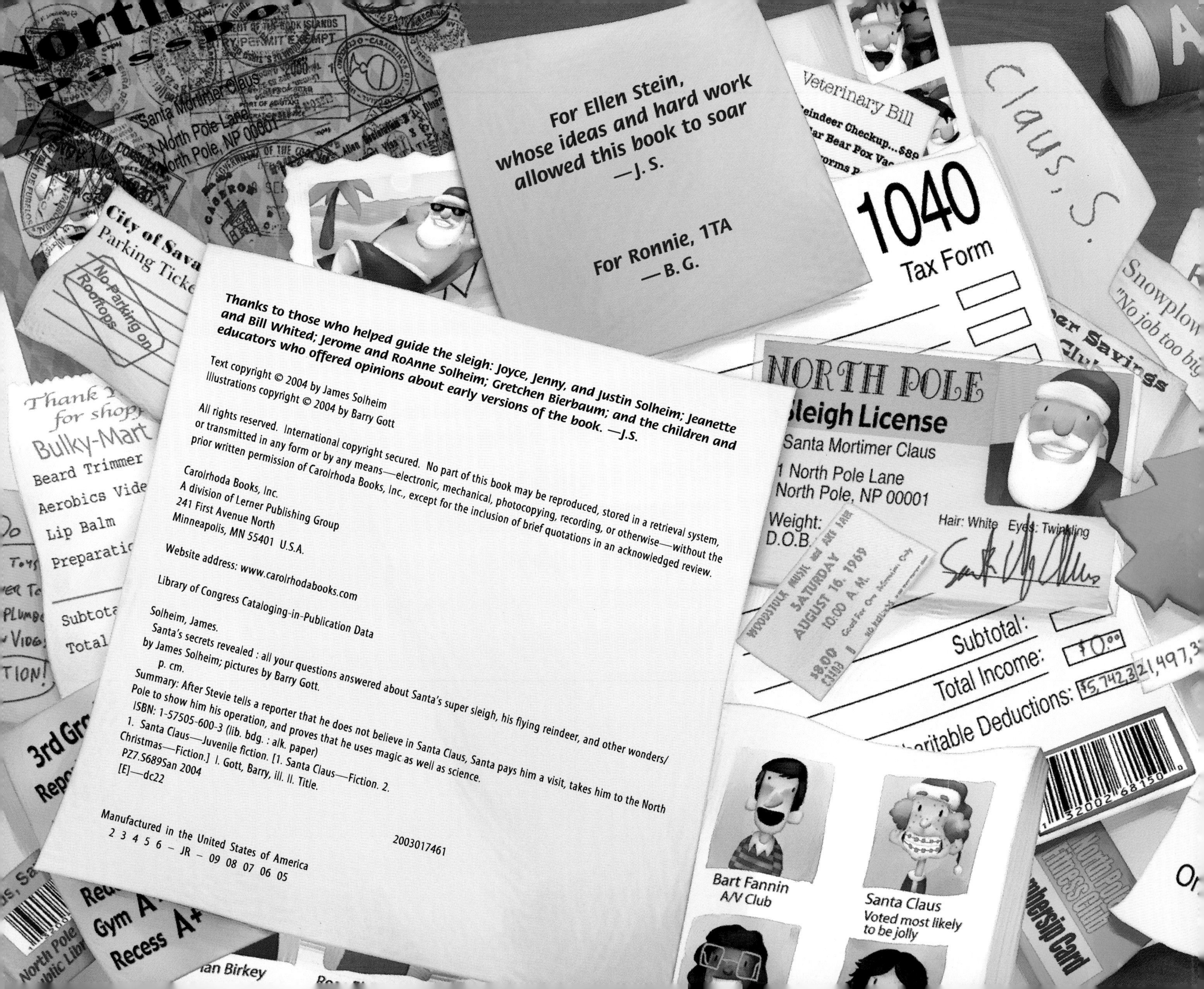

For Ellen Stein,
whose ideas and hard work
allowed this book to soar
—J. S.

For Ronnie, 1TA
—B. G.

Thanks to those who helped guide the sleigh: Joyce, Jenny, and Justin Solheim; Jeanette and Bill Whited; Jerome and RoAnne Solheim; Gretchen Bierbaum; and the children and educators who offered opinions about early versions of the book. —J.S.

Carolrhoda Books, Inc.
A division of Lerner Publishing Group
241 First Avenue North
Minneapolis, MN 55401 U.S.A.

Website address: www.carolrhodabooks.com

Library of Congress Cataloging-in-Publication Data

Solheim, James.
Santa's secrets revealed : all your questions answered about Santa's super sleigh, his flying reindeer, and other wonders/ by James Solheim; pictures by Barry Gott.
p. cm.
Summary: After Stevie tells a reporter that he does not believe in Santa Claus, Santa pays him a visit, takes him to the North Pole to show him his operation, and proves that he uses magic as well as science.
ISBN: 1-57505-600-3 (lib. bdg. : alk. paper)
1. Santa Claus—Juvenile fiction. [1. Santa Claus—Fiction. 2. Christmas—Fiction.] I. Gott, Barry, ill. II. Title.
PZ7.S689San 2004
[E]—dc22
2003017461

Manufactured in the United States of America
2 3 4 5 6 – JR – 09 08 07 06 05

DEC. 25
OMAHA
FINAL EDITION
Comics F24 Sports D1
Santa's Secrets REVEALED
by James Solheim • pictures by Barry Gott
All Your Questions Answered about Santa's Super Sleigh, His Flying Reindeer, and Other Wonders
Children around the world celebrated the news this morning that Santa Claus is, in fact, real. Mr. Claus granted an exclusive interview to Stephen Hossenheimer, Age 8, of Upper Duckwater. Santa explained that he wanted to
Story continued on Page A2
WXMS
Carolrhoda Books, Inc. • Minneapolis
You're Invited
150th annual
Arctic Dry Cleaning
Ticket
One (1) Suit, Red
Hot Chocolate
Marshmallows
Broccoli
Milk
Cookies
Antacid

You're probably wondering about this Santa guy.

Who is he, and how does he keep track of billions of children around the world? Well, I've got the answer to almost any question you can ask about him. That's because I met Mr. Claus—and he told me his biggest secrets!

Last year, I quit believing in Santa. I noticed that our chimney was too skinny for even a chicken to slide down. So when a TV reporter asked me on Christmas Eve if I was watching for Santa, I said,

Are you kidding? Do you really think a 1,700-year-old saint on a flying sleigh brings gifts to everyone on earth—all in one night? And he's got elves on the payroll?

That night, I heard a voice in the dark.

Ho Ho Ho!

Pretending to snore doesn't fool *me*, Stevie. The song has it right—I *do* know when you're sleeping and when you're awake.

Then the lamp clicked on. Beside my bed stood a guy who looked like a giant maraschino cherry with whiskers.

"Dad," I said, "just because you got yourself a Santa suit doesn't mean you have to wake me up. How about leaving the gifts by the tree instead?"

I reached up to give his beard a yank, but then I noticed a... well... an *elf* at the foot of my bed.

"We saw you on TV," the elf said. "What a shame—calling Mr. Claus a fake! But if you go on the late news and say you do believe in Santa, we'll forget about that. We'll even overlook *these* infractions."

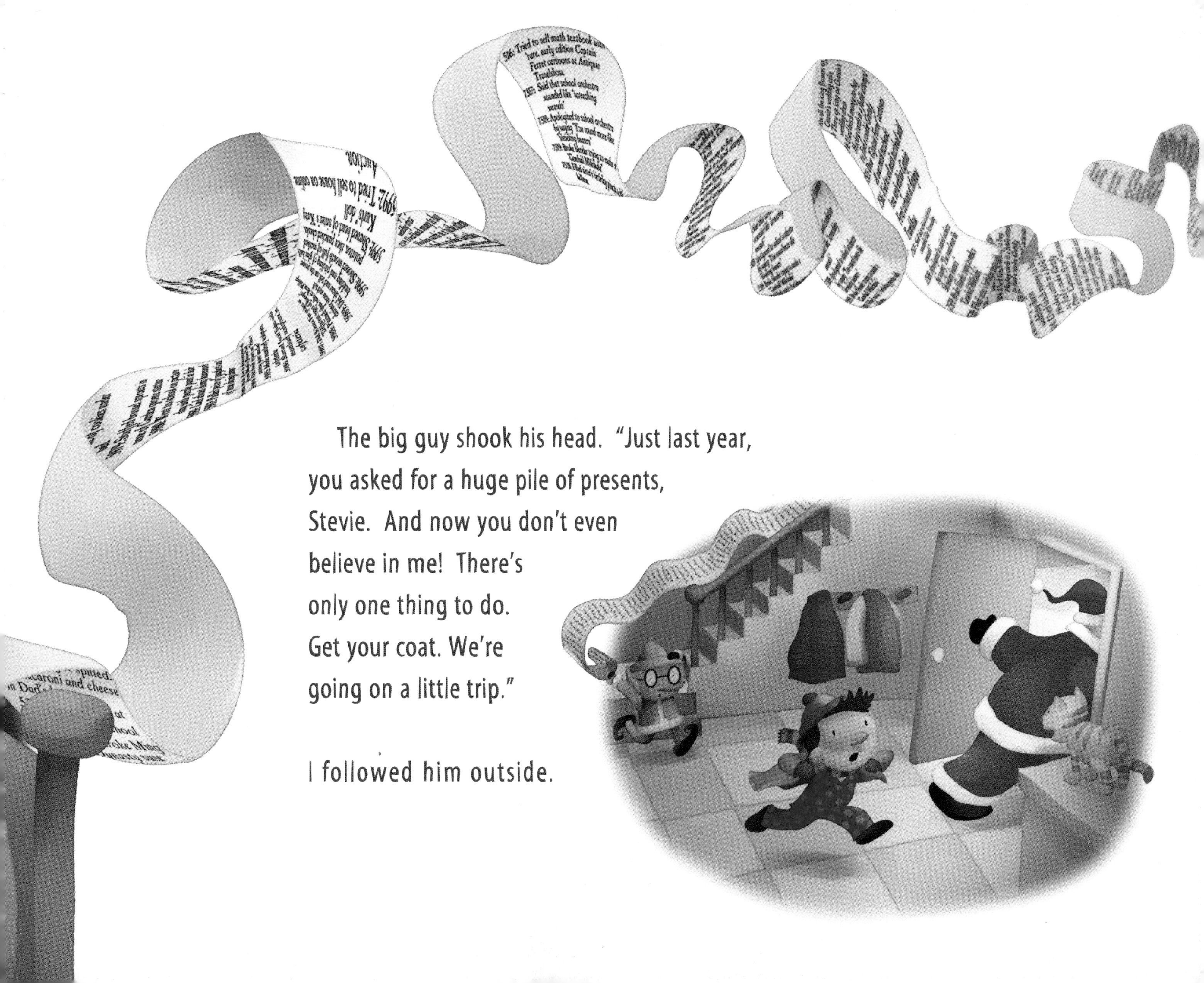

The big guy shook his head. "Just last year, you asked for a huge pile of presents, Stevie. And now you don't even believe in me! There's only one thing to do. Get your coat. We're going on a little trip."

I followed him outside.

Our patio swarmed with elves!

The man in red waved me up into the sleigh. "Seat belts on!" he bellowed.

I looked at the so-called Santa. "Where's your star reindeer?"

"He's home recovering from a bad fruitcake. Harry W. Throckmorton the Dancing Holstein was all they had left at the agency."

With a loud scrape, the sleigh began to move, bumping across our backyard. We barely cleared the fence, thanks to Harry's dance number on the way up.

Flying in the sleigh was like riding a giant dizzy bee.

Cities rolled up over the edge of the earth

as we wobbled and dipped through the air.

But a flying sleigh didn't make a guy Santa. Airplanes once seemed as impossible as Santa's sleigh, and it didn't take a Santa to fly them.

"Your story is so full of holes," I said. "How do you know who's naughty or nice? Or..."

"Patience, Stevie! You'll soon get your answers."

The sleigh slowed down, and the jolly old man swept his arm proudly across the scene.

"Here we are!"

"At the North Pole?" I asked.

"No, Cleveland. Come on—let's see what our spy satellites are picking up."

STOP
Kringle Industries
"Nothing Secret Here"
PAZDURSKI'S Pierogies
Kringle

ELF INTELLIGENCE
EII
INTERNATIONAL
"We know if you've been naughty or nice!"
LITTLE BROTHER IS WATCHING
LOOSE LIPS SINK SLEIGHS
At Santa Industries, we track worldwide naughtiness levels using a string of satellites called PSSSSST! (Papa Santa's Special Super-Secret Satellite Team). Our video cameras are so advanced that they can spot a germ on your ear from 50,000 miles away.
The satellites send videos of every child's behavior to our Cleveland headquarters. Then elves decide who will get toys and who will get lumps of coal.
REINDEER CHOW
COW CHOW
When a child scores a "nice" instead of a "naughty," computers send a command to one of seven Gift Fulfillment Centers around the world. Elves sort the toys into bags that drop into my sleigh as I swoop by on Christmas Eve.

Santa showed me how to check any kid's naughtiness record on the computers. He even typed in my little sister's coordinates so we could aim a spy satellite at her. She was being good, as usual.

Just then, the computers started to spark. Santa typed wildly to bring them under control. "A naughtiness surge is overwhelming the computers!"

An elf rushed up with some papers. "It's been happening all night, sir—every time the TV networks show that kid."

One by one, every TV in the room switched from pictures of kids pulling their sisters' hair or eating with their mouths full to…me! Me on national TV. Me saying I didn't believe in Santa.

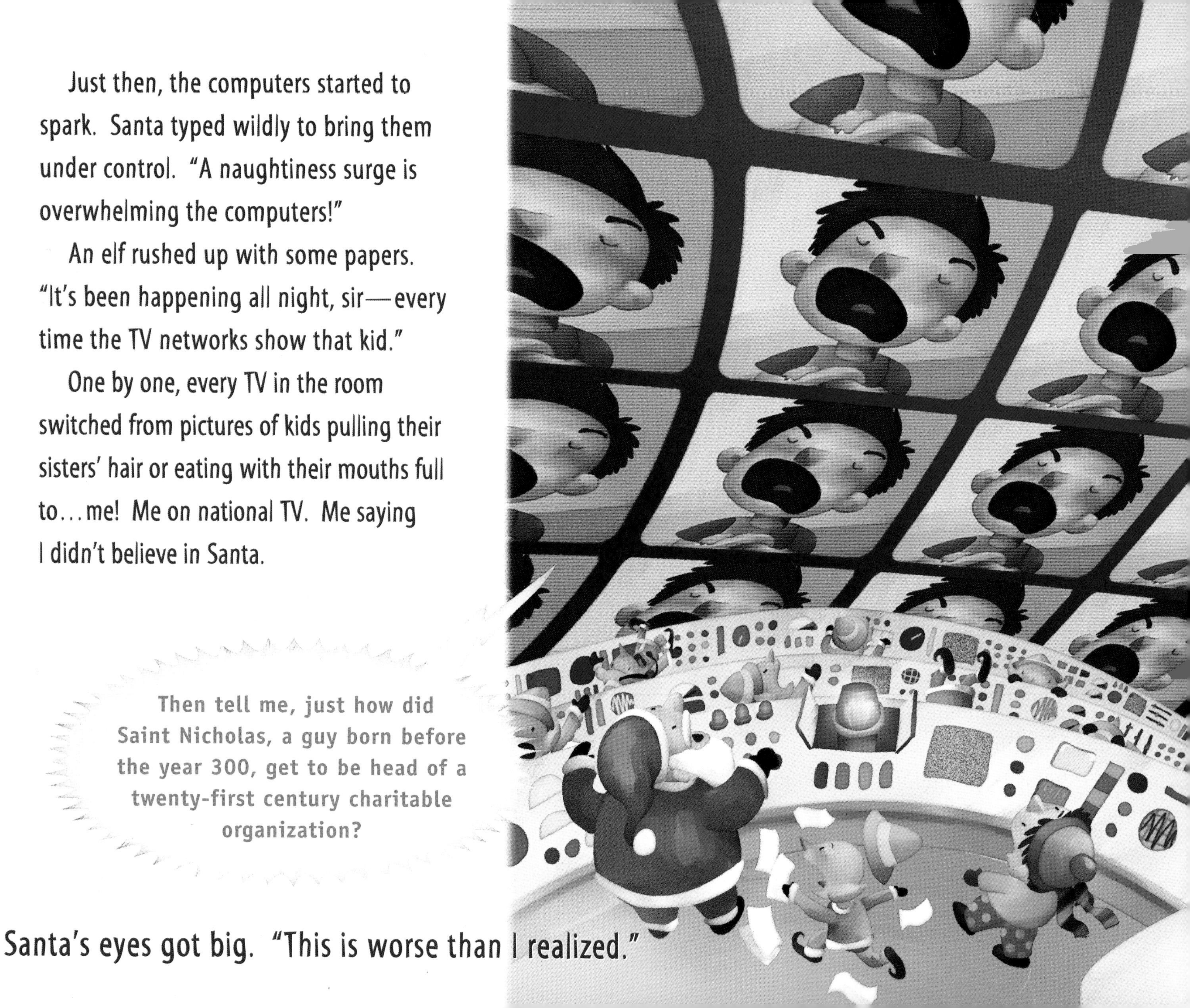

Then tell me, just how did Saint Nicholas, a guy born before the year 300, get to be head of a twenty-first century charitable organization?

Santa's eyes got big. "This is worse than I realized."

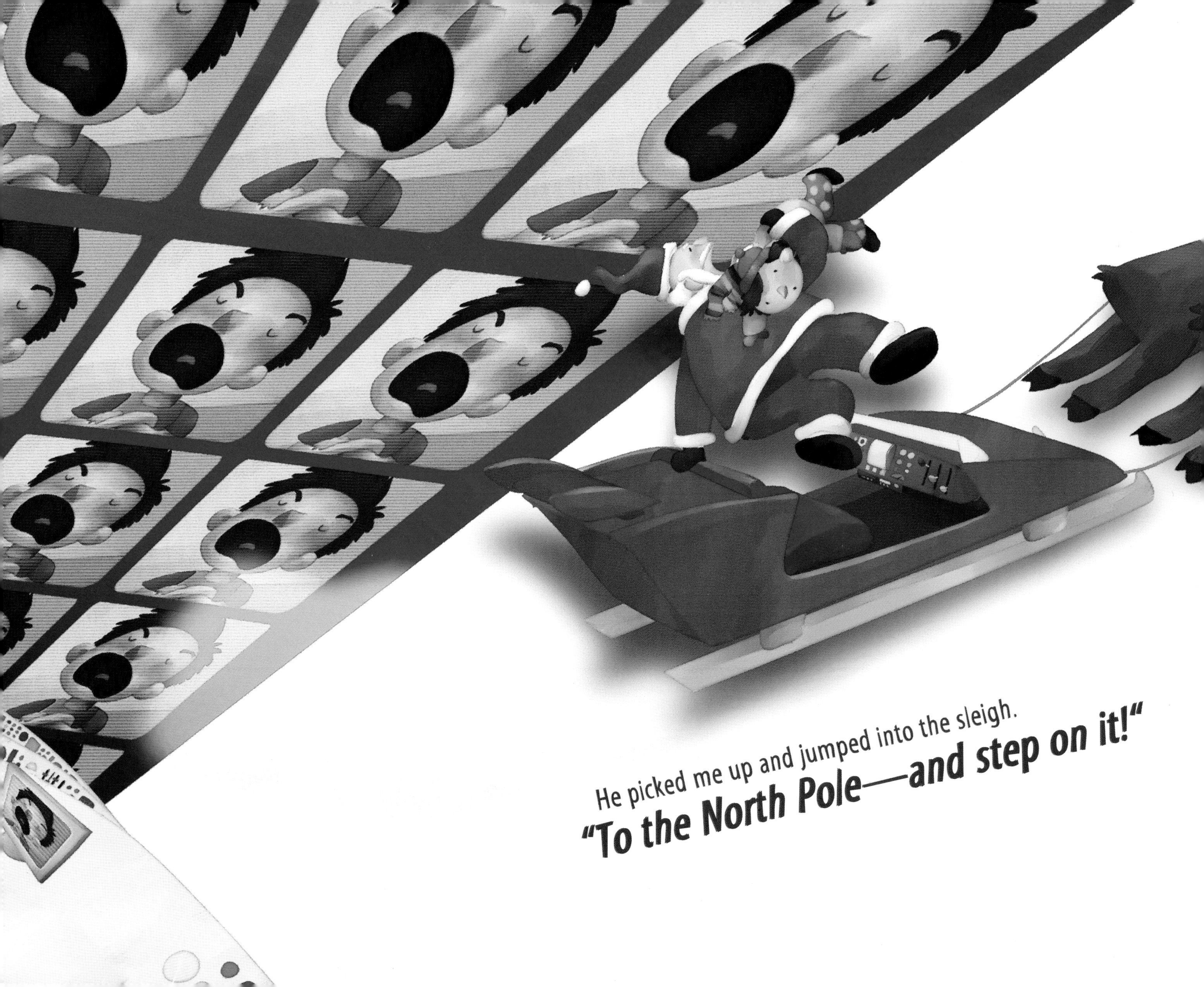

He picked me up and jumped into the sleigh.

"To the North Pole—and step on it!"

In seconds, we were flying high above the earth. The sleigh nearly flipped in a snowstorm over Canada, but we leveled out and rode the wind straight into the northern lights.

Then there it was. The North Pole. Among millions of tiny candy houses stood stores, hospitals, supermarkets, theaters—everything a person could need.

Santa aimed his sleigh at one of the buildings and pressed his garage-door opener.

Inside, dozens of elf scientists floated around the room.

"They're flying—like your reindeer! But how?" I asked.

"Antigravity collars," Santa said. "We're testing our new model."

I grabbed a collar and shot to the ceiling. Surprised, I let go and started to fall.

Just then, a furry flash scooped me out of the air. It was a reindeer wearing a blindfold.

"Don't worry," Santa laughed. "George has radar."

"Radar? You mean you're getting rid of..."

"No, no," Santa smiled. "With radar *and* light, we'll have the safest sleigh in the sky."

Elves, flying reindeer, and now radar. I almost believed that this guy was Santa—but Santa had to be more than satellites and science.

"Okay, so reindeer can fly. And they can give off light and radar waves," I said. "But how can one man deliver billions of toys to the world in one night? Even if you flew to a new house every minute, you still couldn't reach 5,000 children!"

"You get an A+ in math!" Santa said. "But there actually *is* a way to reach all the world's children—the Spacetime Scruncher!"

Santa pulled out a phone. "Honey, can you come over to the labs and explain the Scruncher to a visitor?"

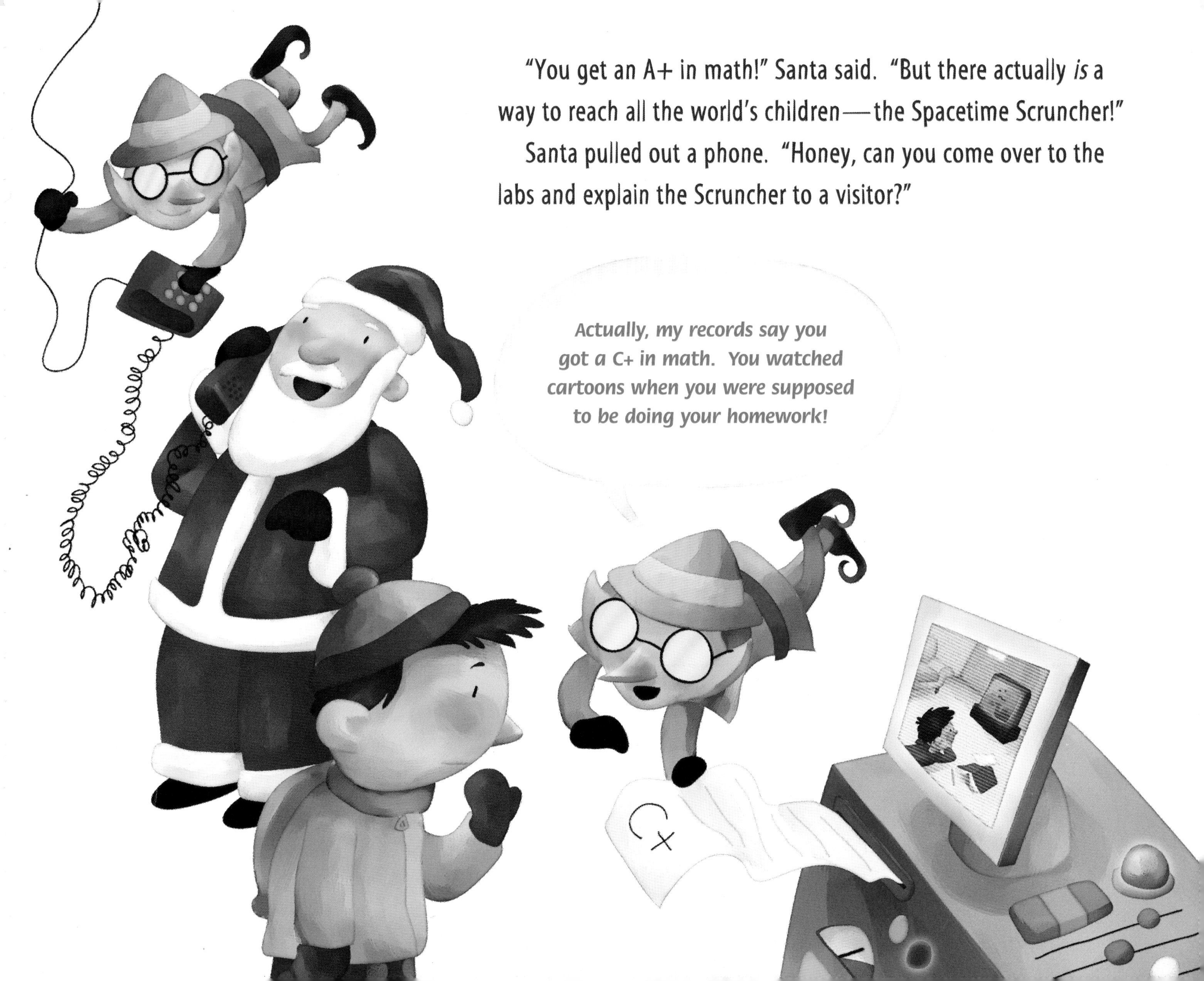

Mrs. Claus didn't look at all like her publicity pictures.

"Old Santa isn't too good with science," she said. "He flies around having all the fun, while I do the work."

"You're the rocket scientist, dear, not me." Santa blushed. "I'm but a simple saint traveling the world and bringing joy to billions."

Mrs. Claus patted his cheek and pointed to a machine on the sleigh. "This is the Spacetime Scruncher," she said. "It sends Santa back in time after each delivery so he can circle the world in one night."

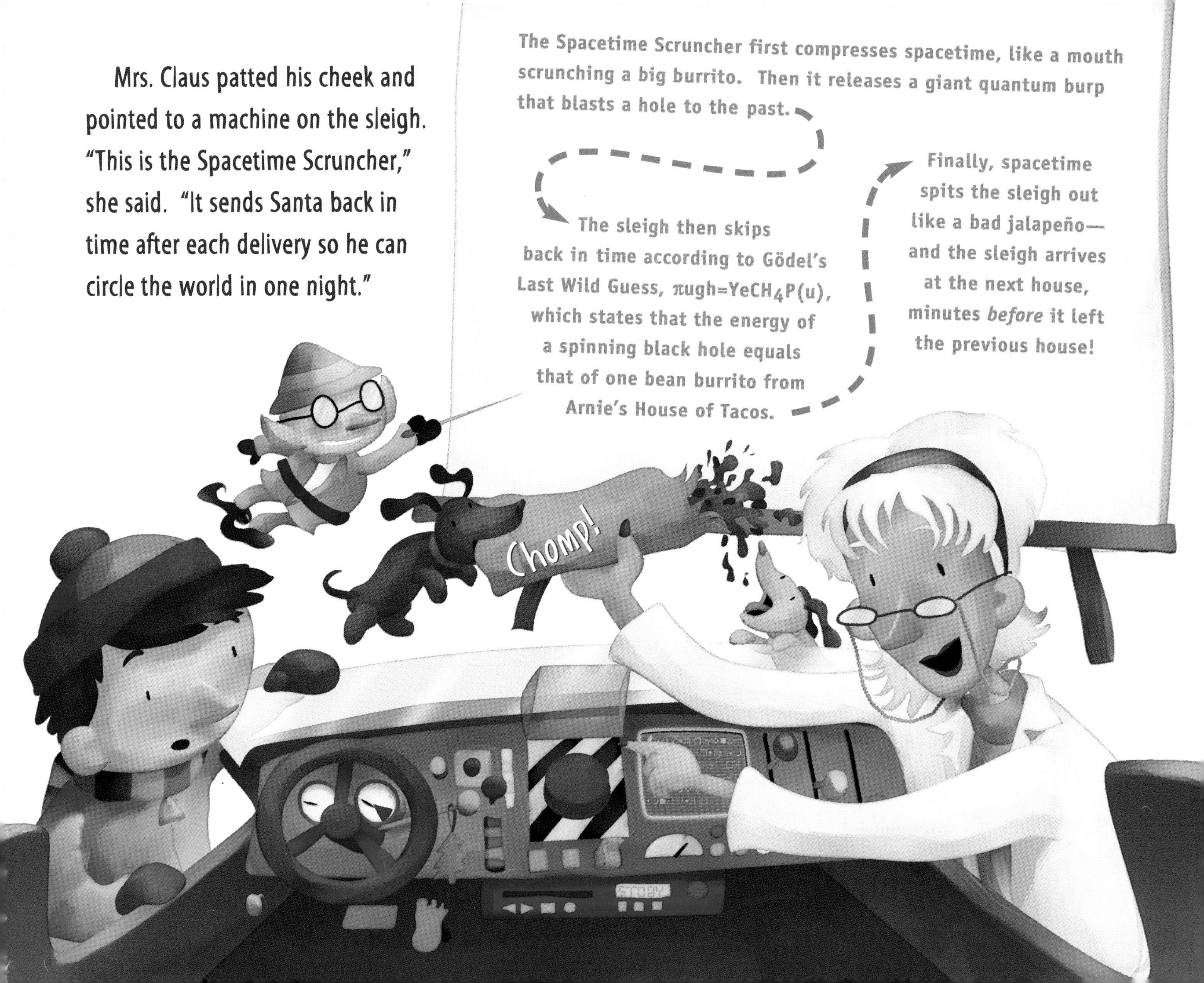

Santa took my hand. "And if you don't believe her, come with me." We piled into the sleigh and whooshed down a tunnel into Santa's workshop.

An enormous bag of toys slid out of a chute and plopped into the sleigh as we zoomed past.

"Yeee-haa!" hollered Santa as the sleigh rocked from the bag's weight. "Get ready to deliver some Christmas joy!"

He shoved the Spacetime Scruncher into high. I saw a flash, and the world stretched to infinity.

We swerved past the pyramids and the Eiffel Tower in the same second. The next thing I knew, we were touching down on a rooftop in Australia.

"Don't you just love Christmas?" Santa hooted.

I started to ask a question, but Santa held up his hand to stop me. "I already know what you're going to say. It's about chimneys and my size, right? Well, watch this!"

With a flash, he became a hopping, bug-sized Santa.

"The Spacetime Scruncher doesn't just scrunch time—it can shrink me too," Santa chirped. "If there's no chimney, I just go in through the keyhole."

Santa jumped into my pocket, and I followed his elf down the chimney. Inside the house, Santa grew back to full size and let me fill up the stockings. He even flipped me a cookie for my effort.

All night, Santa and I circled the world with gifts, landing on mansions and mud huts,

houseboats and houses. I became an expert at scooting down chimneys and climbing up to keyholes.

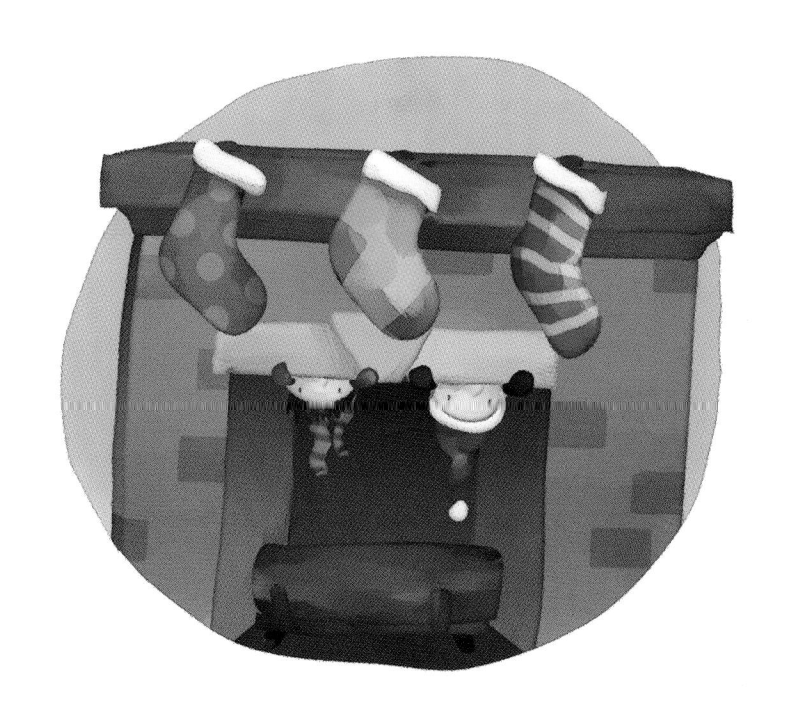

Finally, when the last gift bag lay empty, we landed on a familiar rooftop.

It was my own.

I got out of the sleigh and stood there thinking. Santa had answered every question so far. But I had one more question that I knew he couldn't answer.

You see, I hadn't told anyone what I hoped to get for Christmas. So Santa couldn't give me the toy I really wanted.

"What are you giving *me* for Christmas?" I asked.

"Oh, just a little something," he grinned, pulling a package from under his seat.

Even the reindeer were quiet as I tore off the wrapping paper.

There it was— my present. THE present.

"But how? I never told anyone...."

Santa smiled. "Maybe I've got a little magic in me after all, hmm?"

Slowly a smile grew on my face. Then I went wild—skipping, galloping, shouting to the world, **"Santa's real!"**

Santa pulled me into the sleigh and said, "Now, let's head for the TV networks and set the world right!"

The Scruncher flipped us just far enough into the past to make the late news.

"SANTA'S NO FAKE,"

I said. "He showed me how his sleigh flies, how he circles the world in one night, and... and... you know what? His real secret is magic—good old Christmas magic."

Santa stood behind the cameras, checking worldwide naughtiness levels on his wrist computer. He smiled and nodded.

So if you ever see a jolly gent ringing a bell by a kettle, or a merry gnome sweating in a red wool coat at the mall, just remember—

Santa's the one with the magic.